To my family
and the river gypsies

Bloomsbury Publishing, London, New Delhi, New York and Sydney

First published in Great Britain in 2003 by Bloomsbury Publishing Plc
50 Bedford Square, London, WC1B 3DP

This edition first published in Great Britain in 2014

A CIP catalogue record of this book is available from the British Library

ISBN 978 1 4088 5001 5 (PB)

Printed in China by Leo Paper Products, Heshan, Guangdong

1 3 5 7 9 10 8 6 4 2

All papers used by Bloomsbury Publishing are natural, recyclable products
made from wood grown in well-managed forests.
The manufacturing processes conform to the environmental regulations of the country of origin

www.bloomsbury.com

Marvin Wanted MORE!

Joseph Theobald

BLOOMSBURY

LONDON NEW DELHI NEW YORK SYDNEY

The sheep in the meadow loved
to play together all day long.

But Marvin was feeling rather gloomy.

"What's the matter?" asked Molly.
"I can't run as fast or jump as high as the other sheep,"
grumbled Marvin. "I'm too small, it's not fair."
"But I like you as you are," said Molly.

But Marvin wanted to be just a little bigger.
So when the other sheep had finished eating...

...Marvin ate some more.

As Marvin ate more,
he grew bigger
and bigger...

And soon he could run faster and jump much higher than the other sheep.

But as he grew bigger and bigger
he just wanted more and more...

...until he could not stop!

"Don't eat the forest!" called the other sheep.
"You're getting too big!" cried Molly.

But Marvin loved being bigger.
"Just a **little bit more**," he said.

And he munched up the forest in a matter of minutes!
"That's enough!" shouted Molly.
But Marvin was too busy to listen.

He gobbled up mountains and...

drank whole lakes. But Marvin still wanted **more**...

Then he swallowed an entire country in one big gulp!
But Marvin still wanted just a little bit more...

So he jumped
onto the moon...

and ate the world!

But then Marvin stopped. He was all alone.
He missed the trees, and the meadow, and
the other sheep, but most of all he missed Molly.
And this made him feel very, very ill.

Then all of a sudden...

Marvin was sick.
Out came the world and everything with it.

Although things weren't quite the same
as they were before...

Marvin felt much better.

"I like you just the way you are," whispered Molly.

"I like me just the way I am, too," said Marvin.